Dear Parent:
Your child's love of reading starts here!

Every child learns to read in a different way and at his or her own speed. Some go back and forth between reading levels and read favorite books again and again. Others read through each level in order. You can help your young reader improve and become more confident by encouraging his or her own interests and abilities. From books your child reads with you to the first books he or she reads alone, there are I Can Read Books for every stage of reading:

SHARED READING
Basic language, word repetition, and whimsical illustrations, ideal for sharing with your emergent reader

BEGINNING READING
Short sentences, familiar words, and simple concepts for children eager to read on their own

READING WITH HELP
Engaging stories, longer sentences, and language play for developing readers

READING ALONE
Complex plots, challenging vocabulary, and high-interest topics for the independent reader

ADVANCED READING
Short paragraphs, chapters, and exciting themes for the perfect bridge to chapter books

I Can Read Books have introduced children to the joy of reading since 1957. Featuring award-winning authors and illustrators and a fabulous cast of beloved characters, I Can Read Books set the standard for beginning readers.

A lifetime of discovery begins with the magical words "I Can Read!"

Visit www.icanread.com for information
on enriching your child's reading experience.

I Can Read!

READING 2 WITH HELP

TRANSFORMERS
REVENGE OF THE FALLEN

Rise of the Decepticons

HarperCollins®, ■®, and I Can Read Book® are trademarks of HarperCollins Publishers.

Transformers: Revenge of the Fallen: Rise of the Decepticons
HASBRO and its logo, TRANSFORMERS, the logo and all related characters are trademarks of Hasbro and are used with permission.
© 2009 Hasbro. All Rights Reserved. © 2009 DreamWorks, LLC and Paramount Pictures Corporation. All Rights Reserved. Printed in the
United States of America. No part of this book may be used or reproduced in any manner whatsoever without written permission except in
the case of brief quotations embodied in critical articles and reviews. For information address HarperCollins Children's Books,
a division of HarperCollins Publishers, 1350 Avenue of the Americas, New York, NY 10019.
www.icanread.com

Library of Congress catalog card number: 2008944199
ISBN 978-0-06-172970-6
Typography by John Sazaklis

Rise of the Decepticons

Adapted by Jennifer Frantz

Illustrations by Marcelo Matere

Based on the Screenplay by
Ehren Kruger & Alex Kurtzman & Roberto Orci

HarperCollins*Publishers*

The evil Megatron lost
his last battle
with Optimus Prime,
the leader of the Autobots.

Megatron is the leader
of the Decepticons.
Decepticons and Autobots
are sworn enemies.

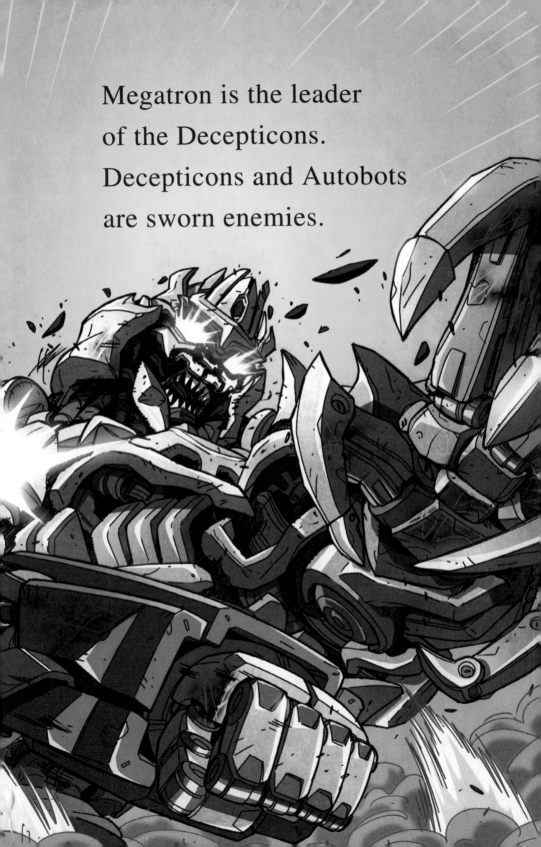

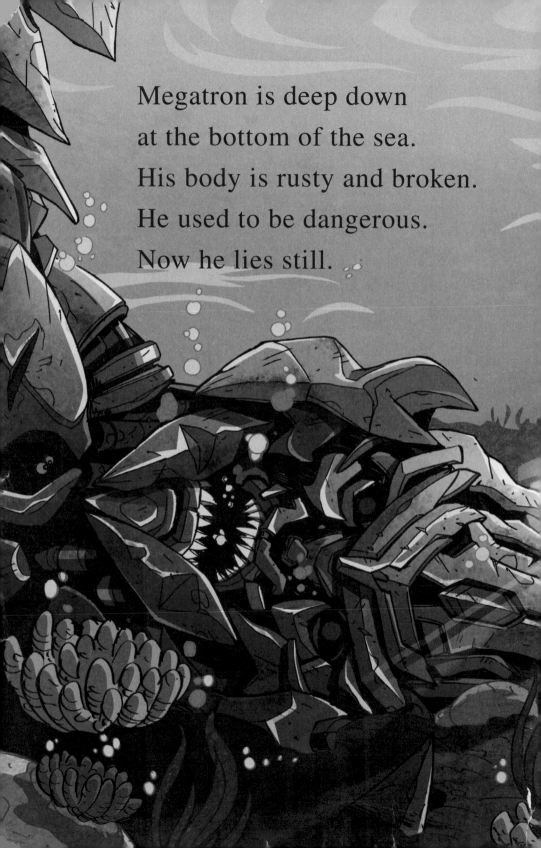

Megatron is deep down
at the bottom of the sea.
His body is rusty and broken.
He used to be dangerous.
Now he lies still.

Humans don't want Megatron
to rise up again.
The Navy watches over him
with submarines.

Megatron's Decepticon forces
want to get their leader back.
Soundwave hacks into
the Navy computers.

Soundwave finds all the top secret
information he needs.

Now the Decepticons can make a plan.

The Decepticons must get
the Allspark shard.
It was the source of
Megatron's energy.

The shard is in a locked vault.
Ravage outsmarts the humans.
He gets the shard!

Now that they have the shard, the Decepticons are ready to go to their leader.

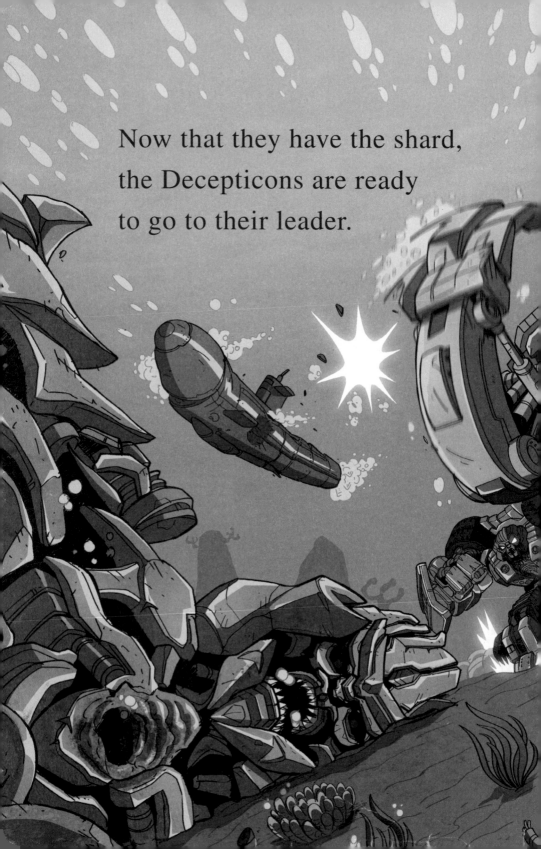

The Decepticons get past
the submarines.
The evil 'bots find Megatron.

The Doctor is a nimble 'bot.
Using his jointed arms,
the Doctor puts the shard
into Megatron.

Megatron bursts to life!

He's back and he's bad.

Now the good guys
have to watch out.
The battle for Earth
has never been harder.

Megatron is not alone.

His Decepticon army is by his side.

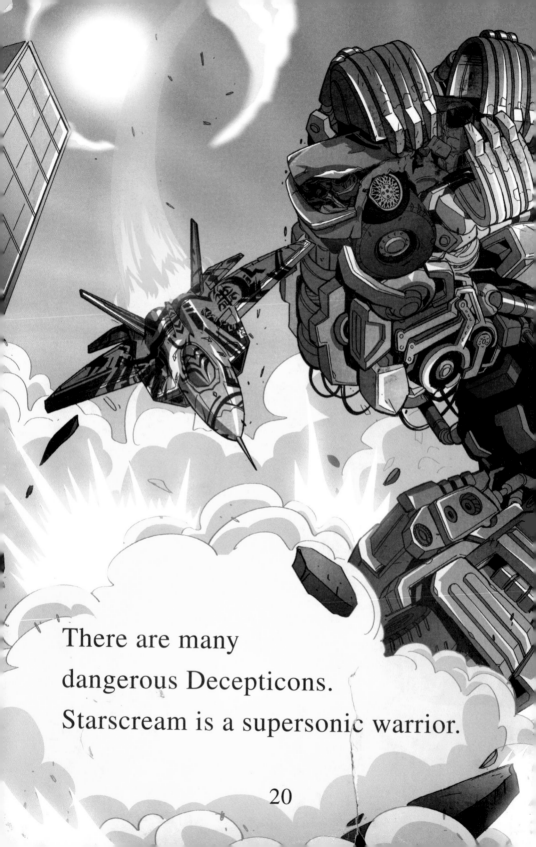

There are many
dangerous Decepticons.
Starscream is a supersonic warrior.

Devastator is one MEGA-bot!

He is a scary foe.

But the most evil Decepticon of all
is The Fallen.
The Fallen has been asleep
for ages.
Now he is back, and he is stronger
than ever!

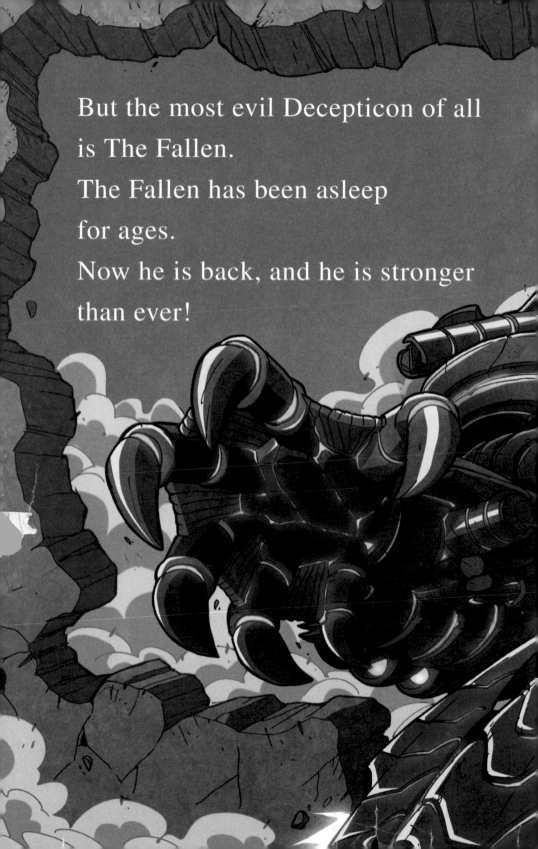

The Autobots
and their human friends
prepare for one hard fight.

Luckily, the Autobots have
two secret weapons.
Wheels and Jetfire are Decepticons
who changed sides.

Now they fight for good
with Optimus Prime
and the Autobots.

Wheels is small,
but he is as brave
as the biggest 'bot.

Jetfire is old,
but he is still very powerful.
He is also very wise.

Can the Autobots beat
the Decepticons once again?

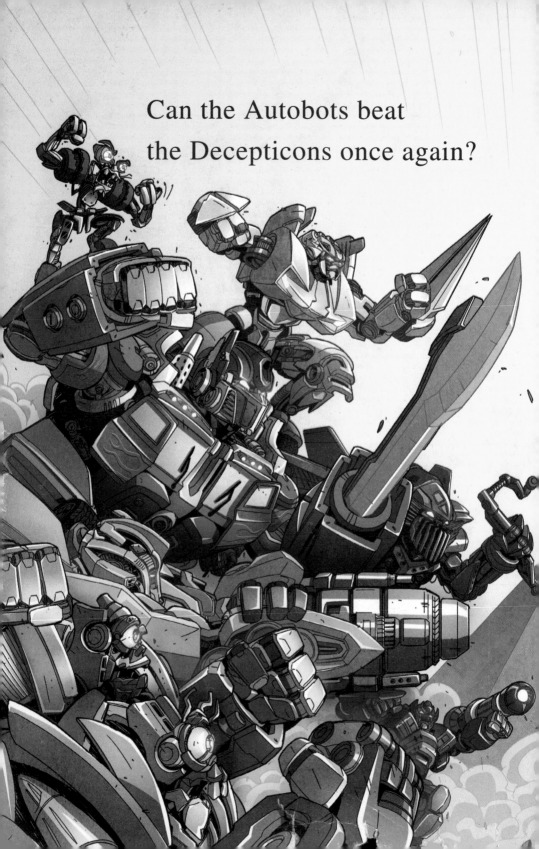

Or will Megatron and The Fallen be too powerful?

Only one thing is sure:
Optimus Prime and his Autobots
will never give up!